A MATTER OF DEATH AND LIFE

Also by Andrey Kurkov in English translation

DEATH AND THE PENGUIN
THE CASE OF THE GENERAL'S THUMB
PENGUIN LOST

Andrey Kurkov

A MATTER OF
DEATH
AND LIFE

Translated from the Russian by
George Bird

THE HARVILL PRESS
LONDON

Published by The Harvill Press, 2005

2 4 6 8 10 9 7 5 3 1

First published with the title *Mily drug, tovarishch pokoynika* by Alterpress, Kiev

First published in Great Britain in 2005 by
The Harvill Press
Random House
20 Vauxhall Bridge Road
London SW1V 2SA

Random House Australia (Pty) Limited
20 Alfred Street, Milsons Point, Sydney,
New South Wales 2061, Australia

Random House New Zealand Limited
18 Poland Road, Glenfield,
Auckland 10, New Zealand

Random House South Africa (Pty) Limited
Endulini, 5A Jubilee Road,
Parktown 2193, South Africa

The Random House Group Limited Reg. No. 954009
www.randomhouse.co.uk

A CIP catalogue record for this book is available from the British Library

ISBN 1 84343 104 1

Typeset in Quadraat by SX Composing DTP, Rayleigh, Essex
Printed and bound in Great Britain by William Clowes Ltd, Beccles, Suffolk

A MATTER OF DEATH AND LIFE

1

If I had smoked, it might have been easier. Then each unfathomable matrimonial sulk could have been followed by a cigarette or two, smoke and nicotine becoming for a while more a distraction than the sense and savour of life – like incense burnt for its own sake – and maybe even helping me discern some glimmer of joy in continued existence. But not having smoked since a boy, to start, aged 30, would have been not only stupid but puerile.

The threat of rain had come to nothing, and it was getting dark. My wife had locked herself in the bathroom as, when actually taking a bath, was her wont. I, prompted by our protracted estrangement, sometimes did the same. At night, we undressed in the dark, and taking a bath by day, were careful not to be seen naked. Naked, one was easily hurt. As she would have agreed. But I, too, was easily hurt, and more often than not, by her. It was not something we talked of any more, though we had once made the effort.

There was a feel of autumn and departing warmth. Time

to be sealing windows and balcony doors. Nature herself prompting thoughts of renewing or bolstering one's comfort, physical and mental. But with us September was of no account. Apart from the occasional remark, we didn't speak. Our coffee, our fried eggs, we made independently of each other.

High time to call a halt. In our one-room flat there was nowhere to get away to.

I never looked from our seventh-floor window without re-experiencing the joy of high-diving, though with no urge to take the plunge. Suicide was not for me. Beyond the bounds of my own daily round, I had a great liking for life. In a state of mild trepidation, I sometimes walked Kreshchatik Street at night studying the faces of the girls waiting for clients on benches or by the fountain near the Friendship Cinema, displaying, in semi-darkness and city street lighting, all the promise of a lurid book jacket. And no great step though it was from imagining myself client, pimp or friend to any of them, it was still a far cry from actually playing the part. Lacking the necessary will, freedom or cash, I got instead a film-like foretaste of life in America, encouraging the hope that similarly sweet images might flicker about me, here in Kiev, take over, and oust past life for the wholly temporary, wholly tedious thing it was in every respect.

2

As a student at the Languages Institute, I'd enjoyed making friends with foreigners, and acquiring, with their speech, a different concept of life. They were as unlike us as mushrooms are to hedgehogs, inwardly as well as outwardly. For them childhood and the games thereof were different. A simple one, popular on and off with generations of children innocent of Soviet rule, I'd been told, was that of establishing a chain of connection between, say, you and the Queen or Prime Minister of England. The principle was ridiculously simple: you knowing him, who knew her, who knew him, until someone personally acquainted with the great Him or Her was arrived at. I gave Brezhnev and Shcherbitsky a try, but no chain developed. Then, thanks no doubt to my general state of desperation, I saw suddenly how to work it here – using killers as links. No shortage of them, and some not all that particular about concealing their activities. Ten or so years back, I'd known at least two – normal, sociable, even helpful types, who had served their sentences. True, the killer was different in those days, had more of an air of romance about him. Now, any kind of relationship is for sale, some have made a lucrative profession of murder, giving us the "contract killer". A term extending the American tradition of image enhancement, whereby "street sweeper" becomes "municipal sanitation operative", the intention being to confer greater self-confidence, greater self-respect. With us, the contract killer was indeed an "operative", a highly skilled murderer working exclusively to order, while at "rat catcher" level, the old-style, romantic, social murderer born of drink or jealousy, remained the common creature he always was. The one who got caught and banged up, while the contract version stayed free as a bird.

For years, in imagination and fantasy, I had been seeking some way out of my dead-end situation in life. And here, on a plate, it was – out of the dead end and of life itself. Too fond of life ever to take my own, I was made for the role of victim. A perfect model of the unfair working of fate: clever man contract-murdered in his prime! How concerned all those who knew me would be, realizing that the me they had drunk wine and coffee with was someone they had never really known – a man caught up in business involving violent showdowns, contract killings. I imagined Criminal Investigation bombarding every one of them with questions. "Had he any enemies?" "What was the nature of his employment?" "Who would have benefited from his death?" and so on. It only remained to find an inexpensive contract killer and the money to pay him, and the ideal murder I had planned would go down as one more unsolved mystery. The idea of an effective end to my senseless life was alluring. One engaging feature of mysterious killings is how often they get referred to in the press and in books, along with names and details, affording a fair chance of survival in the popular memory.

3

Autumn, in the end, was late, tints of red and gold having perhaps proved beyond the means of a nature as bankrupt as the country. True, it was colder and evenings were rainy, but with no vivid turning of leaves. People, on the other hand, were visibly losing their colour, as I, when I looked in the mirror, was mine. Friends telephoned to say how bad they felt. My own ills I kept to myself, as also my own precious plan of escape from the dead end of life.

My wife began to come home later than usual, sometimes after midnight. She undressed in the dark and lay on her side of the divan under her own blanket. These nocturnal homecomings woke and annoyed me, and when not woken I was the more annoyed. She was totally lacking in warmth, something I found infuriating in a woman, particularly when she was in bed beside me.

On Wednesday evening I decided to stay on in town. I had a little money and a fairly clear notion what to spend it on: drink. Only not alone. With one other at least, though better a holy threesome, if all close friends. A boozy night with chance companions was not appealing. At a little before seven I took the metro to Contract Square, where through the windows of a boutique I had twice seen Dima Samorodin, who had been at school with me. We had lost touch with each other since school, and when I had spotted him through the window he had been busy with customers. He would be pleased for me to drop in. We had got on well together, and no bond was more cementing than that of a shared past, whether of school or prison.

Nor was I mistaken. The moment I entered the shop, he hailed me, and while serving, plied me with questions about former classmates. Who I had seen lately? When? Doing what? In response to which, my few chance encounters on public transport sounded tame.

"Give me half an hour," he said. "And when the boss has collected the takings, I'll shut up shop, and we'll have a session."

Rather than wait in the shop, I took a turn around Podol.

The glaring neon of silly café and restaurant names forced withdrawal to the comparative gloom of a bench beneath the monument to Grigory Skovoroda, first Ukrainian Buddhist. On other benches couples were kissing, profiting, as I was not, from the lack of light. Yet why? – being young, agreeable, far from fat? Because no woman was likely to come and ask me to kiss her. Five years back I'd have been doing all the asking to kiss.

When I returned to the boutique, the customers had gone.

"All's well," said Dima. "The boss has been, we can shut up shop."

Drawing the display window curtains and closing the heavy metal door, he cut us off from the world, leaving us as if in a spaceship – and a Western one to judge from the stock of bottles, tins, and the like.

"What shall we drink?" asked Dima, seating me at a small white plastic table and going over to the shelves.

I was reminded of the old "What's the People's is mine".

"Don't be shy – drinks on me," said Dima. "Two bottles a day I'm allowed. Anything over that I pay for at a discount."

"In that case, whisky."

We drank it as others do vodka, in a gulp from small crystal tumblers taken from the shelf for the purpose.

"Zhenka Dolgy, when I last saw him three years ago, was working as a butcher in a food store near the opera. Chemeris has moved to Volgograd. Grown terribly bald recently."

"I did see Galya Kolesnichenko once," I threw in. "Here, in Podol."

Having finished the whisky, we gave gin a go.

"Normally drunk with tonic," said Dima opening the

bottle. "Which we're just out of. Still, it's all right on its own. Remember Melnichuk, Class B?"

"I do."

"Got a death sentence two years ago, but it was commuted to 15 years."

"What for?"

"Taking $5000 protection money off a foreign goods dealer, then chucking a grenade through his window for good measure, killing mum-in-law and the baby."

"Nasty."

We went on to talk of today's crimes and horrors, regaling ourselves with tins of Cyprus olives and Kamchatka crab. Dima's round face grew flushed, his eyes burned bright, and I don't imagine that I myself was a picture of sobriety. Meanwhile we had got onto incomes, the word "pay" having fallen into disuse. Dima made $300 a month plus a bonus in kind, usually consumed with friends – material achievements such as I could not match.

"But my boss, who has five boutiques like this in Podol, plus a currency exchange kiosk, pulls in $5000–$6000 a month," Dima said. "Don't envy him though.

"What would a contract killer make? Any idea?"

"You don't read the *Militia Gazette*. Anything between $5000 and $10,000, depending on how important the target."

"And for a target of no importance?"

"Would there be a market for one?"

I shrugged. "A husband might want his wife's lover removed."

For a moment Dima said nothing, then he, too, shrugged. "Kids' stuff," he said. "No bodyguards, so on the cheap side. Say $500. But no pro would touch it. Certainly none of the ones I know."

With a sigh I replenished our glasses. There was still a refill each left in the bottle.

Alcohol might be coursing in my veins, but my mind was as clear as day.

"So yours has a lover, has she?" asked Dima out of the blue.

"My nod was more automatic than confirmatory, the odds being in favour of her having one.

"I know a chap, bit of a pro," Dima began, lowering his voice. "I could have a word. Decent bloke. Asks nothing up front from people he knows. Got the money, have you?"

"Not at the moment."

"I can provide. Serious stuff, seeing it's family. Like me to have a word?"

"If you would."

4

Two evenings later I looked up Dima at the boutique. There were no customers. The afternoon's drizzle and intermittent rain had clearly sent them scurrying home. He was sitting behind his counter, as in a brightly lit aquarium, reading a book.

"Hello! What's that you're reading?" I asked, entering through the open door.

"James Hadley Chase. Only thing for this weather. How's tricks? Care for a drink?"

I nodded.

Producing an already open bottle of lemon vodka from under the counter, and crystal tumblers, he poured and we drank. For vodka it was smooth, as if concerned to conceal its strength.

"Women's stuff!" declared Dima, seeing my expression. "Hang on while I shut up shop, and then we can talk."

"All OK," he said, resuming his seat behind the counter. "Having just become a father, he's not looking for anything too demanding at the moment, so this lover of yours is just the thing."

"How much does he want?"

"He said $700, but I knocked him down on that. Told him *you* would do the preparatory work."

"Involving what?"

"Target gen. When and where to find him. Maybe a photograph."

The photograph gave pause for thought. So far I had been thinking in the abstract of this so far unseen lover. Whereas it was *me* we were talking about, by God! When and where to find *me*! Calming down and ascribing my slow-wittedness to the weather and the women's stuff we were drinking, I switched my mind back to the matter in hand.

"So what do you think?" Dima asked.

"Fine. I'll get a photograph. How much have you settled for?"

"Ultimately I got him down to $450. So you owe me a bottle."

"When do I meet him?"

"You don't. He'll ring tomorrow evening about passing him what's needed."

Business concluded, conversation flagged, but we sat on, swapping jokes between glasses, for another half hour.

My wife was not back by the time I got home. Making tea, I saw that it was after midnight. Not many windows were still lit in the block opposite. It was wet, the asphalt beneath each street lamp shiny yellow. To cool off, I opened the kitchen window, and poking my head out, gazed down at the deserted street. Five minutes later a clapped-out, foreign-made red car drew up below, from which emerged my wife and a man. For a moment I was afraid they were both coming up to the flat, but after kissing under the light, only she entered the building, and he drove off. I stared at the empty street. So that was him, the target, whose photograph I was supposed to supply. And maybe his was the one I *should* supply – not very original, just common jealousy, for which, given the mutual loss of affection between myself and my wife, there was no need. No, let him live. Let them both live, and enjoy themselves. My contract killing would, I imagined, have some, as yet unforeseeable, effect even on them. A key grated in the lock.

"Not asleep?" she asked without interest but with a hint of surprise.

"Just drinking tea and window gazing."

Making no reply, she swept on into the bedroom.

I waited for her to turn out the light, then followed.

5

The next evening Dima's friend rang, saying he was Kostya, giving me two days to have the photograph and target info. ready, and promising to ring what next.

Next morning I fetched out the shoe box of some long-ditched Jugoslav footware, containing, in random chronological order, photographs of myself at all stages from traditionally naked to in company with tearaway teenage set. Since when, either I had clearly ceased to be sought after, or my friends had tired of photography. I put aside two close-ups: one of me, with a bottle of fortified white wine, in the park at Pushcha-Voditsa, the other picnicking by a camp fire somewhere at Svyatoshino. Checking the photographs against my present self in the mirror, I decided that neither looked anything like me. Somewhere were eight passport-sized photos which I had had taken three years ago in the vain hope of having driving lessons and obtaining a licence.

After a cup of instant coffee, I stuffed the photographs back in the box, and betook myself to the nearest photographer, an old man who kept finding fault with the angle of my chin.

"What's the point in being photographed, if you don't want to look your best?" he exploded at my muttered protest.

When at last he had done clicking the camera on its tripod, he told me to collect the prints in three days' time.

"I'm sorry," I said, "but it must be tomorrow."

"Must?"

"Yes, must."

"Come after lunch then, with a 'thank you'." Not money, that's no use to anyone."

I decided to take a tram to the centre and stroll around for a bit, instead of going home. Much as I have spent my whole life doing, leisurely, aimlessly, popping into this café or that, looking for anyone I knew in the queue.

No sooner did I get to Kreshchatik Street, than I saw what, subconsciously, had inspired my present stroll: the need to gather the target information Kostya had asked for. But to list the cafés I frequented and continue to frequent them, all the time expecting a bullet in the back or the base of my skull, was not the most agreeable of tasks. Not being a masochist, I would have to think of something better, more humane.

So to Great Zhitomir Street and the cellar café adjoining the baker's. It was gloomy and practically empty. I ordered coffee.

By the third cup, my thoughts, deployed for battle, had taken the problem by storm, exciting, as if quite independent of me, even my admiration. Here once more was proof of the essential simplicity of genius. I knew what I had to do, and the relief so offset the effect of caffeine as to let me relax.

It only remained for me to pick the café to be killed in, and when. A public killing was not, of course, an easy matter. Nor was the getaway. But he was the pro, so over to him. Though if he got caught, and it came out that his victim had been an adulterer, bang would go my posthumous reputation, and my death would be more food for gossip than a tragedy. No, escape he must, and his motive be for ever a mystery. Another coffee was called for.

"Another double strength?" asked the coffee machine operator.

"Just ordinary."

I took two lumps instead of my usual one, and set about thinking of, or more precisely, considering every café I knew, before deciding on this one as the least busy towards evening closing time. There would be rarely more than two or three caffeine addicts here then, but on the other hand, he might break his neck on the steep cellar steps dashing for the door. With so much else on my mind, it was curious that I should be so concerned for Kostya whom I had never seen and might never get to see.

6

The old photographer was as good as his word. The photograph was not bad: portrait of the popular actor! The faint, enigmatic smile and the pensive narrowing of eyes were distinctly Leninesque.

It was evening and raining. I was sitting in the kitchen, drinking rosehip tea, and relishing the fact of being alone. My thoughts were of the surprise I was preparing for my wife, not of the new turn in our dysfunctional relationship, which involved her staying out all night and simply popping in next morning to change or to pick up something – so early that I heard, rather than saw, her return.

There was now a touch of both heaven and considerateness in her quitting of the scene. With her about, I could not have been moved to such sentimentality by the evening rain. Some there are whose absence is cause for joy, even happiness. And when your wife happens to be one of them, it's bad.

The ringing of the phone failed to banish the cosy atmosphere.

It was Kostya, telling me that I should next day deposit the needful in Box No. 331 at the sub-post office, top of Vladimir Street, opposite St Andrew's Church.

Weary, I decided it was time for bed, with the rain for a lullaby. But before turning in, I went so far as to take paper and my diary, and select for my demise the following Thursday – a special day, being the one on which I had invited a certain young lady to a café in Podol, which for one whole happy year and a bit had become our "Thursday café". Then as now it had no proper name. On the River

Port tram route three minutes' walk from Contract Square, it had an outer and an inner room, both gloomy and ill-lit. I could have chosen a better, more congenial venue for my death, but this was the one I opted for.

On my sheet of paper I wrote "Thursday, October 12, 1800 hrs, Fraternal Street, café by tram stop 31 (for Post Office Square)", slipped it and my photograph into an envelope, and duty done, went to bed.

7

Tuesday

Next morning I deposited my envelope in Box No. 331.

With two and a half days of life left, it was now a question of how to spend the readily calculable balance of seconds, to say nothing of minutes and hours.

Finished with the post office, I did not feel like going home. We were clearly in for a brief spell of golden autumn weather – red leaves, yellow leaves, crisp, bracing air, cloudless blue sky and not a breath of wind. Heaven, if given to autumns, could hardly better this.

I made for Podol by way of St Andrew's Descent. The galleries and boutiques were just opening. The only sound that of my cheap plastic soles on the cobbles.

Walking aimlessly, I ended up at my Thursday café in Fraternal Street, which happily was open, judging by the student-like creature tucked away in a corner over his first coffee of the day. I, too, bought a small coffee, and sitting at the table in the opposite corner, thought of my remaining minutes and hours of life. I ought, I felt, to take pen and paper and draw up a plan: what to do, who to see, and for once try to manage at least half of it. I had the pen, but not the paper.

The young man had a briefcase.

"You couldn't oblige me with a sheet of paper?"

Without a word he tore a double sheet from a notepad, and as I sat collecting my thoughts over it, rummaged in his briefcase.

"Tuesday, October 10," I wrote, noting it to be 10.30 by my watch.

What to do? Today? Now? The morning seemed wasted already. But thinking of those I would like to see, I saw also the sentimentality of so doing. How to say goodbye, supposedly not knowing that it was goodbye? And to meet up only to talk boringly as per usual was something I had had more than enough of.

But Nina, semi-given-up on marriage, how about her? Always more friends than lovers, we had now and again not been averse to playing lovers also. Ours was a burnt-out passion neither of us wanted to forget. Probably because of the way it had of blazing into life and throwing us into each other's arms, leaving us to drink tea, say it was madness, promising to be in future just good friends. It didn't work, though, and we ended not seeing each other, just telephoning, and that increasingly less often. Chancing to see her coming out of Bonbon, the Magyar café, in the amorous embrace of a handsome, self-assured creature, I saw that part of my life to be over, and a sense of peace ensued that extended to her. I stopped phoning, thinking that was what she would now prefer. She, too, gave up phoning.

"Ring Nina," I wrote on my sheet of paper, and had another coffee.

I found the glaring whiteness of the paper irritating. My urgent concern to make the most of what time I had left seemed suddenly totally devoid of meaning. See who? Ring who? I was needed by no-one, and needed nobody. A fact so obvious as to prompt an icy shiver followed by more positive thoughts, amongst which was the absolute rightness of my decision in favour of suicide. Collecting yet another coffee and taking a colder, more realistic view, I deleted "Ring Nina", and was at last free to devote to myself such time as remained.

The young man at the far table got up and left, and I was alone in the café, the coffee machine operator, Valya, having disappeared into some rear area. The dark interior contributed to the general gloom. Outside, the sun was shining, though to no useful purpose at this time of the year. Still, millions of citizens would be glad of it. Taking pleasure in what served no useful purpose had become a habit, and something I was fond of doing.

On Thursday evening, I would sit nearer the door. To make things easier.

8

Wednesday
Getting up and going to the window I saw that the morning was a swirl of mist, then that my wife had not come home. Hence the feeling of vitality. Ahead lay the task of somehow filling this my last whole day on earth. A walk in the mist, a purely morning phenomenon, did not appeal.

I put the kettle on and sat at the kitchen table. So this was how life ended, I thought suddenly, conscious of counterfeiting old age – as if each day nearer my chosen Thursday marked an advance in my terminal illness.

Tea by a window, a view of mist – as in some luxury Scandinavian clinic for incurables . . . Bergmanesque . . .

This year there would be snow and no me to see it.

But what if there *were* no snow this year, and I missed the fact?

No great loss. Kiev would economise on snow clearing, and that would be that.

My mind was a whirl of trivialities. Nothing of the elevated, the truly philosophical remained. As if I myself had always been trivial and shallow. And as if indeed now the one and only way to become of any account in other people's eyes, if no longer in my own, was by a violent death. Which sounded silly. Clearly my good night's sleep, peaceful awakening and subsequent contemplation of primordially unsullied mist was encouraging silly notions or at least most banal thoughts.

To stop thinking of Thursday, why not write letters to a few long-forgotten friends, touching on the future, and making Friday's tragic news of my death the more poignant?

Leaving my tea, I went in search of a pen and wrote to the young divorcée in Moscow we had got to know while holidaying in the Crimea, exchanging a couple of affectionate letters afterwards.

Dear Tanya,

Forgive my not having written for so long. Life, after quietly disintegrating for the past two years, has now finally gone to bits. No work. No family.

So I'm back at square one again with all paths open. "For the young our land has everywhere a road." In a day or two I'll think about my future. Meanwhile I mourn the past. Not in any very genuine sense, more in the traditional Orthodox manner we carry in our blood. And not exactly mourning – *lamenting* would be the better word. So when, in nine-and-forty days (or is it hours), I've done atoning and all the rest, I shall be thinking of heading Moscow-wards. It would be good to meet up and talk of old times and old friends. If you feel the same, write.

Address as per envelope.

Love, . . .

It practically wrote itself. I could have knocked off a dozen in the same vein, but didn't.

The telephone rang.

It was my wife, drily announcing that she would be coming by car with a colleague to collect her things.

"In the red car?" I asked, but she hung up.

Rather than confront my wife and her "colleague" on this of all days, I quickly dressed, and left.

Still no let-up in the mist. Traffic feeling its way with yellow headlights. People looming strangely out of nowhere, only to dissolve in the general milkiness. A mystical as well as misty start to the day, the dawning of a different, a new world, where all would be well, and whither all might repair who had failed to find a place in the old.

I headed for the city centre with the intention of walking just as far as I could in the mist – to Podol and Fraternal Street. There was, perhaps, no sense in so doing, but with the valiant journeys of Chelyuskin and fellow explorers in mind, I sometimes felt the urge in these less heroic days to achieve, unseen by others, something comparable. Hence, on this last Wednesday of my life, this walk from one end of the city to the other in mist. The reward – a coffee, and coffee was something I would not be having much more of.

Two hours and a bit it took, and when I entered the café and approached the counter, it was, to be honest, with no sense of triumph. Mist deprives one of any sense of space or distance covered.

Out of the greyness into dim lighting. Apparently the first customer of the day, I sat at my favourite table in the corner. Valya had returned to her book behind the tall Hungarian coffee machine.

A girl wearing a leather cap and a shortish, dark grey old-style flying jacket came in.

She had a leather rucksack, and under her arm an artist's portfolio. She brought her coffee to a table beside mine.

I would have liked to speak, make myself known, but seeing her deep in thought, did not.

Drinking up, I left, and roamed further afield in the mist. Though, it need hardly be said, with nothing like the touchingly naively joyous feelings of Wee Hedgehog of the children's cartoon. Still, it cost no great effort to roam, letting one's thoughts do the same. This, my last day, seemed likely to go down as my dullest ever, but I was not bothered.

9

Thursday

By Wednesday evening the mist had either dispersed a bit, or so merged with the darkness as to become less noticeable. Back at the flat, my spirits revived a little. Various bits and pieces of daily life were, I noted, missing, my former wife having, as it were, cleared up after her. Gone was the quartz alarm clock, as also were trinket boxes and hair brushes, leaving the flat just a touch more my own than hitherto. I breathed expansively as I made my round.

That night I had vivid dreams. I could not remember any of them, but so strong was my impression of their vividness, that on waking, I would rather have shut my eyes again and dreamt unmemorably on.

Still, I had something else to think about and get ready for.

I took a bath, shaved, did some ironing – I might have been going to act as witness at a wedding – then settled to my morning coffee.

And before I knew, it was evening, or what passes for it at 4.00 p.m., autumn or winter.

Two hours to go. No mad rush. Nothing more to do. All either done or not needing to be. A sense of elation almost. Proof at last of faith in myself and an ability to be cool and decisive. Not perhaps worth the trouble of a tragic solo performance never intended as a test of ability, but gratifying all the same.

Before leaving the flat, I pocketed my identification document and the letter I had written. For a moment I stood in the passage, wondering what else to take to give whoever turned out my pockets after death some clue as to the nature of the crime. But nothing suggested itself.

I gave the door a farewell bang, aware of the absurdity of so doing. Nerves, clearly.

Outside it was dark and very cold.

Leaving the metro at Contract Square, I passed the Skovoroda memorial with its benches of courting couples. A curious venue for budding or brief romance. Its appeal for the young maybe owing something to the hippy-like way-outness of Skovoroda himself.

But time was getting on and I wanted a double-strength coffee – for me, inveterate café-goer, equivalent of the smoker's last cigarette and just as sacrosanct.

A tram overtook me, shedding feeble yellow light into the blackness of Fraternal Street, until it swung off towards the Dnieper. Again, total blackness, apart from the odd dimly lit window. Only one block to go now, and half an hour in hand.

I slowed my pace. Ten minutes would be enough for coffee.

But Podol blocks were of a length that was quickly walked. I was welcomed by Shufutinsky on tape at much reduced volume. My seat was free. In the small first room, men drinking vodka, and a canoodling couple in the corner. The second room sounded busy. Taking my coffee to my table, I slipped off my watch, and placed it in front of me. The coffee was good and strong, as if Valya, divining it to be my last, had made a special effort.

Fifteen minutes to go. My hands were shaking.

Two girls came in and ordered liqueurs.

"No sitting on over them," said Valya as she served them. "Today's my son's birthday and I'm closing early."

Twelve more minutes.

I drank my coffee and got up to get another.

"Bit shaky, eh?" Valya observed sympathetically. "Overdo it last night?"

I nodded.

"Vodka's the thing for that."

"No money."

"This is on credit," she said, pouring generously.

I thanked her and returned to my table.

"Drink up and go, everyone," Valya announced edgily. It was now 5.55.

The men went like lambs, followed by the inebriated from the inner room.

I sat staring fascinated at the open door through which they all went, but no-one came in.

"Come on now," said Valya standing over me.

I was, I saw, alone in the place.

"One good turn deserves another. My Vasya's 18 today, and I've got the salad to see to."

I drank up, and on my way out collided in the door with a man in a short leather jacket.

"We're shut!" shouted Valya, as I stood aside for him.

"Just one vodka," I heard him say as I walked away.

It was too dark to see the watch I was holding, but it was, I felt sure, 6.00 exactly, and distant chimes confirmed it.

I headed slowly back to Contract Square, listening for any sound of pursuit from the man, wanting to look back, but not daring.

Arrived at the tram turning point, I did look back, but there was no-one.

My fear left me, but so did my other senses.

Mind a blank, doing no more than breathe, I sat on an empty seat at the Skovoroda monument.

How lonely he was up there.

Some were born to be lonely, even in death.

By my watch: 6.40.

Forty minutes of unlooked-for life.

I sat for half an hour or more, then walked up to Kreshchatik Street, and coming on a novice prostitute the worse for drink, took her back to my flat, promising to pay in the morning.

10

Friday

It was a night of dreams, now nightmarish, now idyllic, which depending on whether I was holding in my arms a girl whose name had escaped me, or edging away to the far side of the bed. Next morning I woke with a headache. I got up, leaving my visitor deeply asleep, and sat drinking instant coffee in the kitchen. Several times I looked into the bedroom, only to be surprised by how deeply she was sleeping. The last time I took a closer look at her – we had, after all met in semi-darkness and bearing in mind the state I was in, I couldn't help admiring her courage, and I felt concerned. Before I arrived, she might have been driven off in the car of some sado-masochist!

The logical conclusion was that I had done well, very likely saving her from being beaten up, possibly worse. At which point I remembered promising to pay, though not how much. I felt bad, and glad she was so deeply asleep. Still, something had to be done. I might have to borrow. Borrow? To pay off a prostitute? Had I really sunk that low?

"Hi! Where've you got to?" came a soft sweet voice.

"Like some coffee?" I asked from the doorway.

She stretched, smiling a freckled smile, gave a child-like nod, and placing a pillow behind her back, half sat up in bed.

"It's only instant," I said, going back to the kitchen.

She was beautiful, too beautiful to be a prostitute, and too young. Tumbling to her shoulders, light, once bleached, chestnut hair, slant Tatar eyes, tiny pointed nose, and thin, bright lips which I must have kissed.

"Are you coming?"

"I'm on my way."

Sitting on the edge of the bed, I passed her the cup.

"Any chocolate?" she asked.

I shook my head sadly.

"No matter," she smiled.

It troubled me that I could not remember her name.

"You're nice, but I'm afraid I've forgotten your name."

"As I yours. I'm Tolya."

"I'm really Lena, but out there I'm Vika."

"I like Lena better."

"So that's settled."

It was practically evening when she said she must be going.

I said I would definitely pay her, but at the moment I was broke.

"Forget it," she said with a smile. "Lena doesn't take money, but Vika, if it was her you had wanted, would have charged you $20 . . ."

We kissed.

"You know where to find me," she said from the landing.

"The lift works!" I called, hearing the click of her heels on the stone of staircase.

"Good for it!" she called back.

It was dark. Autumn spreading its gloom. But I didn't care. I was happy. Happy for this my second birth, second breath or something, and the hope it offered for the future.

11

Evening

At about 7.00 the phone rang. It was school friend Dima.

"Bit of a botch-up yesterday. Kostya's been in offering excuses. Got time at the moment?"

"About all I have got."

"Come and have a drink, then."

*

This session went on till midnight. So warm and cosy was the little boutique with a powerful heater and curtains drawn, we might have been sitting by a fire.

As we switched from Hungarian red to a lemon vodka that went well with our feast of cod's liver, it was borne in on me that to taste of life's riches, you really did have to work in a select boutique or be related to someone who did. I was getting the benefit on the score of school friendship and pure luck. School friendships being something most want to forget.

"His watch packed up on him apparently," said Dima, returning, as the vodka warmed within, to the serious. "The long and short of it is, he got there only when they were closing. He's punctuality itself usually. Still, no panic. He'll sort it. Matter of honour. Enough said, then, about that. Life's great! So much to it. Like the girl I got to know yesterday . . ." He shook his head, clearly at a loss for words to do justice to her. "Hairdresser. Love at first sight. Might marry her. Need first to buy a flat."

"I've got a flat," I said. "My wife's left me."

"She'll be back."

"Over my dead body."

"Signed out officially, has she?"

"No."

"It's not yours yet, then. When I get one, I'll see I'm the one registered occupant, and be master in my own house."

He shut up shop, slipped me a farewell bottle of vodka, and we made for the metro.

"If you'd like to earn a bit, I could put something your way," he volunteered as we walked. "Interested?"

"Something dodgy?"

"No more than anything else nowadays. My boss is getting divorced and needs a witness."

"Meaning?"

Dima scratched an ear. "You'd be the one supposed to have slept with her. You attend the hearing, and if they ask, it's 'Yes, I did and hubby caught me,' or words to that effect."

"That's perjury."

"It's a civil case, not a criminal one, and who's to prove

you didn't? She can't, though she may deny it . . . On what you'd be paid, you could booze for a year, and no need to work."

Not an attractive proposition, but with a promise of money not to be got elsewhere, and good money at that. It would mean running foul of the wife. But what the hell?

"If you like, I'll fix a meeting. The boss'll tell you what's needed. Then it's up to you."

"Fine," I said, welcoming the delay.

"I'll give him your number," Dima said, as we parted.

12

Saturday

Dima's boss rang next day, and at 3.00 that afternoon we sat together in my kitchen, he having brought vodka and something to eat. Tall, smooth-shaven, dark, trace of grey, well-trimmed moustache, Sergey was the typical functionary.

"She's cunning," he said, drinking in sips like a man unused to vodka. "Absolute pain. Her lover's someone I know, but don't want to tangle with. It's the morality of the thing – I've a reputation to consider, a future to think about. The odds are, you won't be called. If you are, get up and say your piece. Carefully remembering what most don't know: two birthmarks: left nipple, left buttock."

I listened in silence. Much as I was out to earn money, I wasn't keen on getting into business of that sort. Big money would, I had imagined, involve an element of risk, but there was no obvious risk in this. A few awkward moments, perhaps, but just moments, quickly relegated to the past and forgotten.

"Coming now to the main thing," said Sergey, rubbing his hands as if they were cold, "the rate for the job is $1000. So, yes or no? For me it's urgent."

I swallowed.

"The dollars are yours, whether or not you're called."

I nodded acceptance.

"Come along then."

"Where?"

"Where you and she slept – I'll tell you when – then I'll bring you back."

He drove me in his Opel to Pechersk and an apartment vast enough to get lost in.

"The bedroom," he said, throwing open a plate glass door. "Where, last autumn, you scored, while I – don't you forget – was in the States. That photograph over the bed is Alina. Remember the name."

She was an attractive, heavily made-up blonde.

"That's about it, then. Court appearance Monday, 10.00 a.m. A friend's picking you up. Be ready and waiting."

He drove me home, and for a long while I sat in the kitchen. It was dark. I could have gone to bed, except that I felt too excited and alert, and remained so until 2.00 or 3.00 a.m.

13

The days following my non demise dragged unbelievably. It was difficult to grasp that only two had elapsed since the one on which I was supposed to be murdered, each having extended beyond power of description – the session at Dima's boutique and my meeting with his boss mere droplets in a vast, futile stream of time. I used to like reckoning time on the basis of some expected event – visit, rendezvous or letter. I was not, of course, averse to unexpected letters, but they were chance products and good because not planned for. Now it was Monday I had to look forward to, and acting, for the first time ever, as witness. False witness, to be exact, and the interesting task of performing not the stated role but its precise opposite. Something that was almost second nature to me, as if I were preordained to do. As when I had decided to play victim of contract killer to the full, and chance or Some Other has arranged for me to do the reverse. Why? Could it be that fate was a kind of censorship allowing or forbidding us to do this or that?

So on Monday it was a relief to wake, knowing that something was at last going to happen. It was just before 8.00 when I entered the kitchen, made tea and sat waiting for the car Sergey had promised to send.

The tick of the wall clock was deafening.

Outside it was drizzling. October was the month I liked least – not so much for its Revolution as its wet.

At 9.00 a car hooted, and looking out I saw a Zhiguli. Putting on my jacket, I went down. The middle-aged driver was as silent as the grave.

At the courthouse Sergey told me to wait outside, and when the time came, follow everyone in and stand outside the courtroom until called.

Half an hour later the doors opened, and a whole lot of unsmiling people streamed out into the drizzle, amongst them a lady dressed emphatically in black. Then someone beckoned from the doorway, and Sergey led the way in.

I was standing outside the courtroom as instructed, when a matronly-secretary-like girl in grey check told me to join the others.

"I'm a witness. I was told to wait," I explained.

"Only when it's a criminal case," she said with a smile.

"So in you go and sit near the front."

I sat at the back near the door.

The hearing was brief, and so far as I was concerned, painless. The wife opposed divorce. Sergey, however, began by stating that the co-respondent was present in court and prepared to testify if required. At which, Alina looked nervously around at those present, and kept doing so.

At the end Sergey slipped me an envelope.

"Money for old rope," he said with a laugh, turned on his heel and left me.

Back at the flat, I counted the money: $1000 in $50 and $20 bills. More than I had ever before possessed. I counted and recounted them, laying them out on the kitchen table in hundreds, only to reassemble them in one great wad. My hands were trembling, but this time from joy. I was in funds and could pay off my inconsiderable debts: to the Fraternal Street café for vodka, and to Lena of Kreshchatik Street.

Extracting a $20 bill and wrapping the rest in carrier bag and newspaper, I stuffed it under the bath, not wanting my wife with her key to the flat to cash in on a pleasant surprise.

That evening I took the metro to Kreshchatik Street. There I changed my $20 into the kupon notes that did service for currency during inflation, and with 60 of the 50,000 denomination in my pocket, set off to find Lena.

Last time she'd been on a bench outside the Orbit Cinema. I looked twice, but there was no sign of her. Feeling the cold, I popped into the café-grill opposite the metro station for half a chicken doused in ketchup and 100 grams of vodka, before resuming my search for the girl who had been so easy to get on with.

It was nearly 11.00 before I found her. She looked rather tired, but seeing me, cheered up. We bought two bottles of Amaretto, bars of chocolate and some salami, and repaired to my flat.

We ate and drank, talking frankly and naturally – I of my wife, now off the scene, and my café past; she of liking to be free and disliking her parents and brother. That night and next morning were a great success. For a long while we had no inclination to get up, then at long last I did and brought her coffee and chocolate. Neither of us was in a hurry to go anywhere, but a time came when we ran out of steam a bit, and she, young as she was, had the womanly intuition to get ready and go.

"Like me to ring you?" she asked passing a hand over the dormant receiver of my ancient black telephone.

With alacrity I wrote the number for her.

"If I were you, I'd change the lock," she said, on her way out.

I nodded. She was dead right.

Again she scorned the lift, and I stood listening to the

click of her heels on stone before returning to the flat.

Another autumnal drawing in of the day, but with life now holding the pleasant prospect of her telephoning.

14

Next morning the phone did ring. Only it was Dima, not Lena, urging me to look in that evening. Reluctantly I said I would.

Sickly sun, but dry and evidently bitter cold.

Counting what remained of my kupon notes, I took another $20 from under the bath.

Life went on. A late lunch: tea and chocolate. What I wanted was meat. Shaking out an old shopping bag in which I had brought potatoes from the market a month or more ago, I swept the mess into a corner.

My kupons sufficed in the local food store for a kilo of beef on the bone, a new loaf and a carton of soured milk. Returning to the flat, I found a couple of potatoes and three onions, which I added to the beef to make broth. This I left to simmer, and until it was ready, leafed through old magazines in the living room. At 3.00 I sat down to a plate of broth with crusty bread, followed it with another, and was happy.

The day was drawing in, this time with the parsimony of no street lighting.

So off to Podol and the Fraternal Street café, changing my dollars at Contract Square, and walking the rest of the way.

From the café, a feeble glow of light, voices and laughter.

No queue, and though the first room tables were all taken, there were some free in the inner room. Ordering a large double-strength coffee, I reminded Valya that I owed for vodka.

"Someone was asking for you," she said. "Sounded like a school friend."

"Are you sure?" I asked, remembering that she didn't know my name.

"He had your photograph. Doesn't live here any more, but was passing through and wanted to look you up . . ."

This news came as a shock. For some days I had given no thought to the matter. Taking my coffee through to the inner room and leaving my scarf on a seat, I went back for vodka.

"Lemon- or melon-flavoured?" Valya asked. "I'd go for melon, better taste."

"Melon, then. This school friend, what did he look like?"

She shrugged. "Ordinary. Short. Dark leather jacket. Don't worry. He's either got your address or knows where to find you."

"Did he show anyone else the photograph?"

"He showed it to the three or so who were here. He was in today for a coffee. Didn't mention you, though."

Back at my table, I downed the 100 grams of melon vodka, and thinking it not enough, went back for another 200.

When the café shut, I wandered Podol for an hour, then looked in at Dima's boutique.

"How's it going?" he asked.

"So-so."

"But the richer for $1000, eh?" Broad smile.

I nodded.

"Money when needed! Now you can let it rip!"

"I can."

"Had a drink?"

"A small one."

"Like to join me?"

Locking up, drawing the curtains and producing a bottle, he poured.

"As to your loan, I'm happy to wait, but seeing you're in funds . . ."

I tried to gather my fuddled wits.

With a tut-tut, Dima knocked back his vodka.

"You've been hitting the bottle. The loan is what I paid Kostya for your co-respondent. And to be fair and business-like, 10% of the nice little earner I got you would not come amiss."

"My money's at the flat. I'll settle up tomorrow," I said, downing the vodka and starting to catch on.

"As you like," shrugged Dima, "tomorrow or the day after . . ."

Very soon I was paralytic. Dima found a freelance taxi to see me home. And paralytic as I was, I still saw the $10 Dima slipped the driver.

15

At midday or thereabouts I was woken by the phone.

"Kostya speaking," came a youngish voice. "No trouble. I'm onto him."

He rang off and it took time to grasp what he had said. The game I had stopped thinking about was very much still on.

Two cups of coffee and a cold bath, and I felt better – at least to the extent of thinking more calmly. Several times I went to the window looking for a young man in a black leather jacket, but none of those going about their affairs far below appeared to qualify.

He would hardly show up in broad daylight. Or kill me in front of a crowd. So by day I must be safe.

I no longer wanted to die – my life, though only I could

see it, had taken on a modicum of meaning. I had freedom of action, and my chosen course of a week or so ago no longer suited. I wanted to go on living.

Calmer now and more myself, I took out $550 – my debt to Dima plus his 10% – leaving me much the poorer, but still able to live for a while without thinking of the future.

It was sunny and cold, and on my way to the bus stop I saw that the trees had lost their leaves.

Dima was busy showing an old lady in a long, grey, mangy-collared overcoat a Chinese water pistol. Seeing me, he nodded.

"It's my little grandson's birthday," muttered the old lady, "but there's not much you can buy on a pension, is there?"

"Yours for 250,000," said Dima impatiently. "And that's with 50,000 off."

Pulling from her pocket a bundle of 10,000-kupon notes wrapped in a handkerchief, she began slowly to count them. Dima raised his eyes to the ceiling.

"There's 230,000," said the old lady, adding, "I think I've got some more 1000 s about me somewhere . . ."

"Don't bother! Have it for 230,000!" he insisted, his voice almost a shout, grandly handing her the water pistol, in the manner of one conferring Soviet papers on a person just come of age.

"Thank you, my son, thank you," she muttered, backing her way out.

"Got my goat, she did," sighed Dima.

"Here you are, $550 which includes your 10%," I said, handing over the dollars.

"Steady on," he said, "you're doing yourself."

"How so?"

"The $450 owing leaves you with $550, 10% of which is $55."

I shrugged.

"Never did care for double taxation," he said, producing from under the counter an opened bottle of Hungarian Palinka and two small crystal glasses. "Not put out, are you?"

"Sorry, no – just been having a bit of a bad time recently."

"So may you now be in for a good one," he said, raising his glass.

And suddenly, more clearly than ever, I felt that I was.

"A word of advice," said Dima. "Those dollars of yours should be put to work. You've your life ahead of you. You need money to live. Several ways of going about it – the least troublesome is to let them earn you monthly interest. Don't buy shares, that's watching your money run off with. I can put you in touch with people who will give you 10%. What they do is lend at 15%, securing against property. So long as the mug pays his 15%, it's 10% to you and 5% to them. If he doesn't, they seize his flat or his garage, and sell. You get your 10%, they get 200%. They do the work, you do bugger all, just sit with a book."

I promised to think about it.

"When are you going to live a proper life, that's the question," Dima observed gently, pouring us another.

It was daylight by the time I got home. I put my change from Dima on the kitchen table, then undressed.

My fear now was of the dark.

The situation I had got myself into had a certain wry humour about it. Here I was, by chance, still alive, while still being stalked as per plan, and with no idea how to stop being. Make a clean breast of it all to Dima? Get him to pay off Kostya and put an end to it. Then it would come out how I had been fooling him about my wife's having a lover, him and Kostya, making pawns of them both. No, I must either find some other way, or let it drag on, just living from one day to the next. Not an attractive prospect, now I was valuing each day of life so.

It was getting dark. I wanted to go and collect Lena from Kreshchatik Street, but wanting even more to live, I sat waiting for her to ring.

Half an hour later she did, saying she was coming and would I meet her from the metro. Yes, I said, and only when the receiver was back on its rest, did I consider the implication of what I had promised. My sense of self-preservation was obviously in abeyance. So much so that while dressing I had no qualms about going out into the night where, lurking behind the next tree or around the next corner, might be a man in a black leather jacket.

I did, however, experience a thrill of fear walking to the bus stop, ear cocked suspiciously at the most ordinary of night sounds. The two hundred metres from my block to the bus stop sapped me of energy and left me sweating, as if I'd been running flat out. The ten minutes by bus to the metro let me regain my breath.

Walking back to the flat from the bus stop hand in hand with Lena, I felt more confident. Being in company made it less frightening.

We spent the night making love, only breaking off to lie in the dark and talk, or, just as comforting, stay pressed together, not talking.

"Would you marry me?" Lena asked out of the blue with a note of irony.

"I think I'd rather adopt you."

She laughed. "Then you'd get put in prison."

Her laughter in the dark was sweet and reassuring.

Towards morning, as she lay peacefully asleep, curled up like a child, I wondered why it should be that with her beside me I felt self-assurance return. Maybe because I saw her as guardian angel, or guardian angel-cum-bodyguard, protecting me with her goodness, creating a kind of invisible, protective layer around me – as much a biosphere to me as I was to her.

"Bodyguard angel," I murmured with a smile, which she was.

I reached out to her, and sleepy protests notwithstanding, drew her to me, and fell asleep, feeling wholly and utterly safe.

16

That afternoon, when alone again, I gave serious thought to my security, fuelling it with the purchase of an *Advertiser*, in which, under SERVICES and among any number of plumbers and parquet floor specialists, I found two security firms, and dialled the first.

"TOPSEC, can I help you?" came a pleasant female voice.

"I could need a bodyguard. What do I have to do?"

"Come and draw up an agreement."

"What do you charge?"

"Tariffs vary, depending on the degree of service, from $50 up."

"$50 a month?"

"$50 a day."

Thanking her, I rang off. At that price, ten days was the most I could afford, and then what?

Settling myself in a chair, I scanned the adverts, a soothing occupation creating an impression of normality: here a builder of dachas and houses, there a breeder of coypus, there a grower of roses, and under LONELY HEARTS, good nonsmokers and teetotallers seeking others of their ilk – a world one would gladly dwell in for ever.

Then, amongst those desirous of buying what they did not have or selling what they did, I lighted on something quite out of the bourgeois mould: "Highly dangerous missions undertaken for appropriate fee." No telephone number, just an address: Irpen, 87, Soviet Street.

Next morning, standing in a filthy coach stripped by vandals of its seats, I took the electric line to Irpen. I quickly found Soviet Street, and ten minutes later arrived at a gate bearing the number 87. The house, approached through a long-neglected garden, was old and similarly neglected. I knocked at a sheet-iron reinforced door.

For a while, no response. Some glass object fell, rolled over a wooden floor. Footsteps followed.

"Yes?" said a husky voice.

"I've come about the advert."

An unshaven, puffy-faced man in his early forties opened, took a deep breath of the fresh air, and came alive.

"Come in," he said, and shutting the door behind me, I followed him.

The room had lace runners on every surface, a photograph of an elderly couple on the wall, and a musty smell.

"So?" he said, seating himself at the table which was covered with a lace-edged cloth.

"Tolya," I said, extending my hand.

"Vanya," he responded. "So?"

Stifling a certain irritation, I got down to business. "Someone's trying to kill me."

Grunt of disbelief.

Feeling more stupidly placed than I was already, I got up to go.

"What's up?" he asked in surprise. "I'm listening."

"You talk and I'll listen," I suggested, thoroughly piqued.

"What about?"

"You. What you do."

"Officer rank, Afghan war. As to what, anything: guard consignments, bring in German cars, rough up as required . . . "

The husky voice was in keeping with his appearance and scanty attire – striped vest, tracksuit trousers with the Dynamo stripe.

"So, how about it?"

"I'm on," he said, suddenly serious and businesslike.

"How much?"

"$500, if no insurance," he said sizing me up.

"Bit steep."

"$400, then."

"$350," I persisted, hardened by haggling with those lid thumbed lifts from.

"Done," he said. "Shoot."

A former business partner out to settle old scores, I explained, skipping pre-history and giving Valya's description of him.

"Expects to find you in the café, right? OK. Do I get an advance?"

I shook my head.

Smoothing a bristly cheek, he seemed not to mind.

Five minutes later, lean face even leaner, scratching an armpit, and gazing at the ceiling, he said, "No problem."

"Meaning?"

"We lure him to the bait."

"Meaning?"

"It's you he's after, so we get him as he comes."

I saw the logic, but wasn't struck.

"Look, if he's sitting concealed somewhere, it's not me he'll go for – I don't exist – but you."

"And what if he gets me?"

"He won't, not while I'm there. I've a plan. Tomorrow show me the café, and we'll fix things on the spot."

We agreed to meet in Podol the next day at 11.00.

17

Vanya turned up on the dot of 11.00, a different man, clean shaven, in jeans and quilted anorak.

"So?" he said, and to Fraternal Street we went.

The café had only just opened. Would we like a vodka? Valya asked. The coffee machine would be ten minutes heating up.

"Not when working," Vanya said.

I sat at my corner table. Vanya had a look at the other room.

"Y-e-e-s," he said, joining me. Then with a "Won't be a tick", got up and went out.

Valya disappeared into the back. The coffee machine did its heating almost soundlessly. The street door was shut. I tried, in my solitude, to breathe more or less soundlessly.

The door banged open, and a horse-faced man in grubby beige jacket and black knitted hat looked in.

I shrank into my corner.

"Valya, need more vodka?" he bawled.

"Still got some. Could do with a case of Amaretto," she said, appearing from the rear regions.

The man nodded and left.

"Double strength?" Valya asked, having checked the machine.

"Please."

"How about your friend?"

"No idea."

"I'll wait till he comes."

I took my coffee to a table.

The silence was unnerving.

Something was missing, something as essential as hydrogen to water's oxygen.

"Valya," I called, using her name for the first time ever, "How about some music?"

"Shufutinsky?"

"Is he all you've got?"

She went through her tapes.

"There's Allegrova, Alyona Apina, Kirkorov, Gadyukin Brothers . . ."

Liking Apina's freckles as seen on TV, I opted for her.

"Only not too loud."

"Damn all to eat you gave me, but promised me the world . . ." Apina sang. I relaxed. The coffee did wonders.

Again the door banged open, but less alarmingly. It was Vanya.

"Like a coffee?"

"No, let's go."

I followed him to a courtyard adjoining the café, a run-down area with the remains of a Zhiguli and a rubbish collection hut, backed by the walls of a three-storeyed building, now a chaos of beams and rubble.

"Every day now, from five till closing time, what we do is sit in that café at different tables," said Vanya. "When he arrives, you come out for a piss behind this hut. He follows, I follow him. OK?"

"Fine."

"And have the dollars to settle up on the spot, so as that's the last we see of each other."

I still wasn't struck, but there was obviously no sense in arguing. He was in command, and seemed to know better than I what to do.

"Starting from when?" I asked.

"Today. The less I see of that electric line the better. Café at five, then."

★

I had a bath, ate, put my feet up, and thought about the evening. The notion of playing worm on hook to catch a big fish was demeaning.

Time dragged.

At four, when I set off, it was almost dark.

My usual place being taken, I sat with my double strength nearer the counter.

Vanya, for all his "not when working", was sitting with a glass and a bottle of beer by the door.

No Kostya.

My second double strength left a bitter taste. To dispel which I switched to melon-flavoured vodka. Time became winged.

Just short of 7.00, Valya shooed customers out.

Vanya and I were the last to leave.

"Head for the metro," he whispered.

My steps rang out in the darkness, belying all efforts to walk quietly. A left turn along the white wall of the Mogila Academy, and fifty metres ahead, Contract Square, bright with street lamps and headlights.

"Same place, five tomorrow," said Vanya, overtaking and darting into the metro.

18

The third evening found me bored with playing bait. The very sight of coffee brought a bitter taste to my mouth, so, waiting and noting who came in, I opted for something stronger and more relaxing. Two possible Kostyas presented themselves, and I'd once been on the point of slipping out, until, buying a bottle of vodka, the suspect retired to the inner room, only to be escorted out half an hour later by two proletarian types just as drunk as he.

At 6.40 a third leather-jacketed young man appeared, paused in the doorway and looked round, before going up to the counter.

Two women sitting opposite got up and went out. I looked across to where Vanya was sitting with his beer. Vanya looked back, drumming his fingers on the table.

Song and tape came to an end, and in the silence that followed I heard rain. Which, having no umbrella, was the last thing I needed!

"Would you drink up, please," Valya called, before setting Shufutinsky going.

The new arrival sat down opposite me, and putting his coffee on the table before him, playfully revolved the cup by its handle. His leather jacket was completely dry. Evidently the rain had only just started.

Suddenly a hard stare in my direction, and I was no longer in any doubt that this was Kostya.

"Got the time?" he asked.

"Five to seven."

With a nod of thanks, he returned his gaze to his cup.

Had he not deliberately sat himself at my table, I would

not have been so terrified, and my legs so a-tremble.

Some insects, it occurred to me, feigned death in the face of danger. But much good would that do me.

Again he was staring, now tight-lipped.

Thinking of what? Or simply attuning himself to what lay ahead?

A point came when I knew that if I did not get to my feet now, I never would.

Must go for a pee, must go for a pee! I kept telling myself, struggling to break free from paralysing fear.

When I did at last get to my feet, I saw a jerk of his hand slop the coffee he was about to gulp.

Trying not to rush, I walked from the café into the rain, and ten metres later turned into the courtyard picked by Vanya.

The rain made it impossible to tell whether or not I was being followed. In the courtyard I was at bay, in total darkness, noisily treading something underfoot.

Relying more on memory than my eyes, I got to the rubbish collection hut and froze. Then, cautious, hesitant footsteps.

With my blood running cold, I edged around to the back of the hut, and again stopped dead, mindful of the money I had about me, uncertain whom I had the more to fear: Kostya, or my advance-waiving bodyguard.

Over bricks and bottles I somehow scrambled to the

doorway of the derelict house, slipped inside, and squatted down, breathing hard.

Again, a crunching of glass, then, over and above the gentler swish of rain, long minutes of silence.

Something hit the ground with a thud, then again silence.

"Hi!" called Vanya, flashing a torch. "Let's be having you!"

He lit the way for me, and when I got to him, shone his torch on the prone figure of Kostya.

"Care to settle?"

He checked the amount, and turning the body over, retrieved the hunting knife driven to its hilt in Kostya's breast, wiped it on a rag, and concealed it about his person. Unzipping Kostya's jacket, he took from his waistband a silenced automatic.

"So now," he declared, concealing it as swiftly as the knife, "it's back to square one, and over to you."

His departing footsteps were soon drowned by a fresh downpour.

When at last I made a move, it was, without knowing why, to stoop and transfer the contents of Kostya's pockets to my own.

Back at the flat, I shed my drenched clothing in the passage, and took a hot bath.

My aim was to cleanse myself of the past and the whole of what had just occurred. But I hadn't the strength. Either

I had reverted to drunkenness, or I was sickening for flu. My head throbbed. I just managed to dry myself and flop into bed.

19

It was getting on for midday when I awoke. My head felt as if I was indeed sickening for flu, but I appeared to have no temperature. With an effort I got up and into a tracksuit.

Lying in the passage where I had dumped them, were my muddy, still-wet clothing and jacket. Running a bath, I threw socks, sweater, jeans and jacket in – after first emptying its pockets onto the kitchen table – adding a half packet of soap powder for good measure.

Waiting for the kettle to boil, and later over my tea, I examined the contents of Kostya's wallet: $50, kupon notes, photograph of wife, sick and weary looking as if newly delivered of the tiny baby in her arms. There was also a folded envelope addressed to Konstantin Shustenko, Flat 325, 22, Victory Avenue, Kiev, postmarked Moscow and bearing an illegible scrawl in lieu of address of sender, which I laid aside unread. So that was who Kostya was. Not that it made any difference.

Echoing strangely in my head, the ringing of the tele-phone. I lifted the receiver.

"At last!" cried Lena. "Hi! I've been ringing for days. Where've you been?"

"Away."

"Like me to come over?"

"Yes, except I've got a cold or something . . ."

"I don't mind, if you don't. Be there in an hour."

Returning to the kitchen, I put Kostya's belongings into a carrier bag and the bag into the cupboard.

She took less than an hour.

"Look," I warned, "what if it *is* flu?"

Attempting to cure whatever it was by love, she caught it herself, and we lay at death's door together, coughing and taking our temperatures. Being ill together was better than being ill alone, especially as Lena managed to get us something to eat and brew tea and honey. A week, and we felt better.

"My people'll be ringing round the mortuaries for me," she confessed one evening.

"Give them a call."

Reluctantly she did.

"Hi! It's me. Still alive. See you," she said and rang off. She then volunteered to pop round to the food store, we having eaten everything there was.

We dined, just short of midnight. Meat with wine.

We slept in each other's arms for warmth.

A gale set the windows rattling. I dreamt of blizzards.

20

"Illness over, so that's it," said Lena after breakfast. She dressed, packed her diminutive leather rucksack, said she'd ring, and sallied forth, pausing on the landing to blow me a kiss.

She was gone, like the flu. It was the first Tuesday in November. I was on my own again. Winter was on its way. There were two tentative falls of snow that quickly thawed.

Looking from my window, I felt as if I had dropped out of the march of time and needed to catch up. But how?

Opting for simplicity, I betook myself to the reading room of the Housing Office Library, and sitting next to a nosy old pensioner, looked through the last fortnight's newspapers. And on the back page of *Evening Kiev* I spotted, framed in black, condolences for one Shustenko, Nikolay Grigorievich, sometime Chief Engineer, Artyom Works, on the tragic death of his son, Konstantin. The *Kiev Gazette* for the same date went into where and how he had been murdered. The militia were treating it as a vengeance killing directed at the father, currently Chairman of the

Independent Real Estate Exchange. There had been an attempt to blow up his car, followed by two arson attacks on his flat.

The Kiev criminal news for the other days was in the same vein: murders, bombings, roughings-up – the daily norm of any big city.

So I'd not missed much being ill. The only difference was the weather. And the snow which I had never thought to see again.

To mark my continuing hold on life, I decided to go to my Fraternal Street café.

Apart from the rather strange girl I had seen once before, in black leather cap and shortish flying jacket, with artist's portfolio, it was empty.

"Would you care for a vodka?" I asked.

"I would," she said, looking up, "and some chocolate if there is any."

Bringing another 100 grams for myself, I sat down for a chat, but after downing the vodka and pocketing the chocolate, she made ready to go.

"Sorry to rush, but I live way out at Borshchagovka," she said.

She was Anya, in her final year at the Institute of Arts, of which I had once heard that no-one normal got accepted there. Still, it's the abnormal who are the more interesting. Dangerous company they may be, but never boring.

At 6.30 Valya made plain that it was time I took myself off.

It was snowing.

21

The November 7 celebrations passed unnoticed, although next evening as I entered the block I found a medal-bedecked veteran, last of the Mohicans, standing incapably drunk and as if for ever at the door of the lift.

I had got home feeling cold, only to discover that the flat was, too.

Throwing off my quilted anorak, I set to work. Last year we had draught-proofed at the beginning of October, when my wife had been in charge, quietly suggesting what should be done, and rather than endure sulky silence, I had done it. This year winter had caught me on the hop, in an on-my-own state happily punctuated by the comings and goings of Lena.

My divorce case proceeds were dwindling. Kostya's $50 were still safe in his wallet, and likely to remain there when what I had was gone. They were not mine to touch. Like the other souvenirs of that rainy night, which now and then I laid out on the table, still not reading the letter, but studying the photograph of the weary wife with her baby. Now she would be even wearier.

Sometimes it seemed that these were things I had found and should be taking back to the address on the envelope. Going through Kostya's pockets was something I had forgotten, though not the fact of having done so. I kept having the strange sensation that what had happened had been nothing to do with me. I had simply been walking along, found the wallet lying in the street, and now had to return it. I could do it by post.

I would sit drinking tea, looking at the photograph of mother and child. In this whole affair she was the one innocent victim. The child was, too, but it would be some years before it became aware of the fact. Of Kostya I thought less often. His chosen employment would have been the death of him sooner or later. In a sense, lives would have been saved by his early death. Or would they? No. His death would merely provide additional employment for his fellow hit men.

I made up a paste, stuffed foam rubber into the gaps around the window frames, and stuck strips of newspaper over. Half an hour and the job was done. No draughts, but it was no warmer. Still, everything takes time – heat from my radiators especially.

Drinking tea in the kitchen, I looked out at the cold, uncommunicative winter evening.

Tomorrow children would be snowballing, grown-ups telephoning the militia to collect from the bus stop the frozen corpse of a drunk. Winter I endured in much the spirit of a ferryman waiting for his river to unfreeze.

What, I wondered, would Kostya's widow be thinking about, also perhaps gazing out of the window, baby asleep beside her, as snug and warm as she was cold and lonely.

Maybe one day I would get to know her. "By chance." After all, I had her photograph and address. If it so fell out, I would try to help in some way.

And what was *my* wife doing now? Where? Who with?

No, no problem there – she wouldn't be lonely.

Weighed down with weariness and a craving for warmth, I went to bed.

22

Several days passed. The flat warmed up, and was cosy to return to from −15°C outside. So for the greater part I stayed in, drinking tea and reading the same old free *Advertisers*, which was dull. My days consisted simply and solely of waiting for Lena to ring. We had not seen each other for a week. Usually she rang towards evening, but this time it was noon when she called. She was at home with a lousy cold, and would call me when she was better.

Before I had time to wallow in self-pity, the telephone rang again. Dima. "Come tonight and have a glass or two."

Eight p.m. saw us shut in the little boutique, warmed by an electric fire. Dima laid out the usual fare, switched on a cassette player, and poured lemon vodka.

"Heard what happened to Kostya?" he asked after our second glass.

"I saw in the *Gazette*."

"Seeing that he didn't do the job, he owes you."

"So what, now he's no more?" I asked, uneasy lest my voice betray me. Dima stared, licking his fat lips as if they were dry. So convinced was I that he knew, that I poured myself another and drained it at a gulp.

Reaching into an inner pocket of his denim jacket, he kept his hand there so long that I felt suddenly I was past caring. What must be, must be, and if tackled, I'd tell the truth.

His hand, when eventually it emerged, held some dollar bills which he laid on the table.

"Kostya and I worked on trust," he said, still staring. "He was never one for cash in advance. So now I'll have a word with someone else if you like."

"No longer any need."

He nodded, sighed and drank.

"Were you and he on friendly terms?" I asked.

"No such thing nowadays. Just business relationships. Kostya was trustworthy. Nice bloke. Still, can't be helped. That's life. Another will take his place."

Repeating the phrase to myself, I wondered what exactly he meant. The words doubled their meaning, even deconstructed themselves. It was nothing whatsoever to do with the lemon vodka. Just the richness of Turgenev's "great and mighty" Russian language asserting itself.

Disconcertingly sober, I poured myself another, and one for Dima, although he was already well gone.

The dollars were nearer his hand than mine. Better for them not to have been there at all, claiming my attention in a way that Dima's half-closed eyes were humorously aware of. Taking a larger glass and pouring in the contents of his own, he filled it from the bottle, and with a wry grin and a "Down the hatch!" drank the lot. Then, screwing a $20 bill into a ball, he sniffed it.

I didn't respond. Maybe I wasn't expected to. Dima was drunk, too far gone to be caught up with. All I wanted was to go home and sleep.

23

I surfaced late next wintry morning with no headache, surprisingly fresh, but hard put to recall more than snippets of my conversation with Dima. But there, in my jacket pocket, were the dollars, screwed up $20 bill included. How, Dima being drunker than me, they had got there, God alone knew.

Beyond my frost-patterned windows fluffy snow flakes were falling.

Breakfast. To tick of wall clock and boiling of kettle, I munched a sausage sandwich, feeling at peace. Dima knew nothing. How could he? And now I could safely ask further about Kostya and his wife of the haunting face, whom, reality yielding to fancy, I felt sure I knew already.

Cold shrinks, reduces volume. I remembered that much from physics at school. A precept that seemingly embraced the non-physical, now that winter was shortening, compressing my day, making me spend most of it at home in the warm. Winter, clearly, deepened a sense of loneliness, loneliness not being governed by the laws of physics.

Loneliness was now the air I breathed, taking charge of my dreams, foisting the same one on me several times in succession, turning nights of repose into moralistic object lessons. These dreams, like TV soaps, had their themes, their heroes and a certain attractive, ethereal, green-eyed, blonde heroine, of whom, when no longer dreaming, it was a relief to be rid of. It was not that I preferred reality to dreams, rather the reality of imagination to the animated cartoon.

For if life be no more than to contend with loneliness, then what cheaper and more dependable form of alleviation than imagination?

As I drank my tea, my thoughts were of her to whom I felt so deeply obligated, while knowing nothing of her, not even her name.

*

That evening I went to Podol to see Dima and glean what I could about the family that, as a result of my recent depression, was a family no longer. It was still snowing. The fluffy, leisurely flakes created a Christmas fairy-tale aura of tranquillity.

In the small area between the two rows of kiosks and boutiques more people were about than usual. Nearing Dima's boutique, I stopped dead in horror – it was now no more than a burnt-out shell drifted over with snow, exciting the curiosity of passers by. "Burned down this morning," said a bent old woman with an astrakhan collar.

"I saw it . Young fellow chucks in a bottle of petrol, his mate flips his cigarette after it, and whoosh! Up it goes, and out rushes the assistant, jacket ablaze, and rolls in the snow."

Again my world had shrunk, contracted, and to next to nothing. I had no idea where to find Dima, having neither his address nor his telephone number.

Soon tiring of watching the snow efface all traces of the fire, I set off for Fraternal Street, in search of the familiar.

The café was quiet. My table was taken by a silent elderly couple, quaffing vodka as if their lives depended on it. They were smartly dressed. Maybe they had suffered some misfortune.

Valya greeted me with a smile.

I sat over 100 grams of vodka until the café closed.

24

Days passed. No-one rang. With amazing persistence a never-ending torrent of snow floated down in feathery flakes past the window.

As often as I stopped to look, the sight enthralled me but sent thought scuttling into hiding, as if in fear, leaving me to confront the torrent more in the manner of an animal – a wolf or hare – than a human being. Something within me died, and I might stand ten or 15 minutes at the window until distracted by some sound or other. At which point the ordinary thinking human that was me would revive and put the kettle on for tea, think thoughts again and shape his mood accordingly. Usually it was his loneliness that he thought about, and those who might have rescued him, extricated him from it, but hadn't. Then women in general, and this on the strength of his believing Woman's sacred duty always to have been to combat Man's loneliness. The moment would come for a deep sigh and a cry of "Rubbish!". And in the lull that followed, into his mind's eye would steal the image of a woman he knew, and was not averse, even a little glad, to see appear. One that he dwelt on and carried with him.

The snow whirled, and my sense of loneliness mounted infinitely faster than small coins in the piggy-bank Father gave me as a child. I remembered breaking it open, and helped by Father, reckoning up my capital. I remembered, too, Mother's loud, mannishly coarse complaint that that wasn't enough for half a new piggy-bank.

My thoughts turned to the dollars given back to me by Dima. As I put them on the table, I felt suddenly that I must wash my hands. It was a physical urge, more on the part of my hands than myself, a dichotomy so ridiculous as to prompt a smile. Washing one's hands after handling money – dollars at that! – savoured of the puke-making, moral reading prescribed in a distant past in the pages of the *Literary Gazette*.

Calmer, I did in the end wash my hands before considering the dollars further. After long trying to decide not so much where I stood regarding them, as where they stood regarding me, I hit on words that said it all: *they were someone else's, not mine.* And at once all stress vanished, the unpleasant sensation in my fingers ceased.

Dirty money it might be, but what money, other than the freshly printed, wasn't? The fate of any currency being to pass through the hands of rogues, criminals and bribe-takers. So, ownership established, to restore it was now only a question of time and of resolution on my part.

It was still snowing. And I was thinking no longer of the money, but of the woman who was unaware that it was hers. The woman of the photograph beside me and my cooling cup of tea.

Night was descending over the city, together with the snow.

25

Two further days of snow and loneliness, during which I finally resolved to discharge a real, if self-appointed, duty.

The dollars from Dima and the $50 from Kostya's wallet I put into an envelope on which I wrote the latter's address.

At midday, I set out to walk, expecting to take about an hour and a half.

Face smarting from the intense cold, I walked slowly, having lost something of my initial resolve, and was not sorry to see a food store with cafeteria and people drinking coffee. I went in and joined the queue.

The coffee was stewed and would have been better left undrunk, but masochistically I took my time over it.

Arriving at the block and finding the right door, I hoped that there would be no-one on the other side of the blue-painted plywood. I pressed the bell, intending to wait only a minute.

Footsteps. Inspection of my tense expectant self through the spyhole, then a woman's voice asking guardedly, "Who do you want?"

The question caught me unawares, and the distorting spyhole would not have shown me to advantage.

"I'm a friend of Kostya's," I said uncertainly.

The door opened a little, and there was the face of the photograph, fresh-complexioned, not in the least weary, reddish brown hair shoulder-length and silky. Her long black skirt and bright red blouse suggested, to my relief, that she was on the point of going out.

"I owe him money . . . I'm sorry, I don't know your name."

"Marina," she said, extending a hand.

"Tolya."

"Come in," she said. "But quietly – Misha's asleep."

We made our way to the kitchen.

"Would you like some coffee?"

I said I would, adding that I had been sorry to hear what had happened to Kostya, and that it must be hard for her.

Turning from the stove, she looked at me wide-eyed.

"It's funny," she said slowly and wearily, "but you are the very first to offer condolences. Any number of people phoned when he died, but only to confirm that he had. As if they thought there was some trick about it. And when I said that he had, end of story – no commiseration, no inquiry after us . . . Did you know him well?"

"To be honest, no. Only through business . . ." I laid my envelope on the table. "But he was always reliable . . . Always ready to help . . ."

For a while there was silence, then she sat down opposite me, and we drank our coffee. She looked at the envelope, and then inside.

I expected some reaction – gratitude, if not verbal then in manner – but there was none.

"It's difficult, very difficult without him," she said slowly, looking into her cup. "It wasn't always easy when he was here, but nothing like this. Now I'm stuck here like a caged animal. Baby can't go out in this weather, and

I can't go out and leave him. Kostya's parents don't ring. Thinking I hate them now he's dead."

"Maybe I could help."

"Very kind," she said. "Things will be easier once we're through the winter."

She was far more beautiful than the black-and-white photograph had suggested. But the fatigue I had seen in her face was still there, in the way she spoke, moved and sat at the table.

Finishing my coffee, I got to my feet.

"May I leave my phone number – in case you need any help?"

She thanked me, and I wrote it in her book.

It occurred to me, as I walked away, that I had failed to get her number. Glancing back at the five-storey Khrushchev-era block, I tried to decide which of the third-floor windows were hers, but could not. I had not noticed what they looked out on. Still, that was not important. Any more than not having her telephone number. Maybe she would ring me. I walked on.

26

It had not till now occurred to me that duty done and a debt repaid might have some effect on mood, so notional a concept being the stuff of the young revolutionary and legend. "Debt", when not of the financial kind, had been a word delivered with a touch of sarcasm. Financial debt was something I had always tried to avoid. Now, in my thirtieth year, here was the word acquiring its full and conventional meaning for me, a me not only easy in mind, but also experiencing a new sense of satisfaction or contentment. And on the strength of this sense of a duty discharged, albeit in monetary guise, I began to think well of myself. Which may have been why I started the day unusually early, mooching about my one-room flat, bursting with energy and at a loss what to do with it.

It was dark, but day was breaking, hastened by the appearance of lights in the block opposite.

A new day was dawning.

And I felt a need for something new. But what? New life? New sensations? No idea. New illusions, more likely.

I watched it growing light. Nature was raising the curtain on a new day, presaging, I felt increasingly certain, a fresh beginning.

A cloudless, bluish sky, and, though not yet visible from my window, a gentle yellow sun bringing a sparkle to the snow. No lights opposite any longer. My watch showed 9.45. The day fell short of expectations, but that evening Lena rang.

"Better?" I asked.

"Yes. Miss me?"

"Been terribly lonely."

She sounded happily surprised.

"Really? All right to come?"

I would have preferred the usual "Be there in an hour" calling for no response.

"Of course."

"Something funny about your voice today," she said. "Be there in an hour."

I sat at the kitchen table and waited, with growing eagerness to see and hold her. Angry at my long solitude without her, I had forgiven her within ten minutes of her call. Forgiven her on the score of her still wanting me. Maybe she thought the same way about being wanted by me. And here was evidence. But the on-off nature of our relationship – her never-seen but operative timetable of appearances and disappearances – prompted anxiety as to the fragile, short-term nature of it. Her double life and double name suggested less than full value in our love-making, but so what? "All or nothing" being not much of a slogan, since nothing was what you usually got in the end. Not that I was ready to dedicate myself to anyone whole-heartedly, even a woman.

Hearing the bell I sprang to my feet and ran to the door with surprising impatience.

"Just let me get my things off," she laughed, as we kissed in the doorway. "There's no rush."

Her long black jacket with fur-trimmed hood went onto a hook, and there, in black slacks and emerald sweater, she was.

"So you missed me?"

My missing duly assuaged, she produced champagne and a bag of food, and we took ourselves to the kitchen. The salami, baguette, butter and Turkish pastries she set out on the table were welcome indeed after a fortnight of sausage sandwiches and the occasional luxury of fried potato.

"Relief aid!" I said. "Thank you."

She smiled.

"Not much use hungry, are you?"

"And when my hunger's satisfied?"

"We'll see. When did you last have a proper meal?"

"Way back, but I've got by."

"Right, knives and forks – any potatoes?"

"A couple of kilos."

"Right. Today's a holiday, but tomorrow you get some more in. Stick the champagne in the fridge, top shelf, if there's space."

"My fridge is all space," I said opening it.

"What a way to live!"

Half an hour and the meal was ready. Rising to the occasion, I got out two good glasses.

"All we need are a few flowers," she said dreamily, contemplating the table. "Something you've never given me."

"Never knowing when to expect you."

We began with champagne.

"What's the toast?" I asked, raising my glass.

"Us," said Lena, "and our not being ill!"

Fried potatoes, thin slices of salami, fresh, crusty baguette and butter – a celebration for stomach and spirits, filling the little flat with a riot of happiness.

"Does your cassette player work?" she asked.

"Should do. It's ages since I tried."

I put the tape on in the living room and came back. The music was a little while starting, and when it did, my forkful of salami stopped dead in mid air, just short of my mouth. I looked at her in amazement. She smiled, gestured helplessly.

"Corelli. The B-side's got rap, *Car Men*, Bulanova, if you'd rather . . ."

"No, I like it. Just surprised."

"Not sure if I do or not. I just sometimes feel I must hear it. Pure music is like a tonic. It soothes when I'm feeling neurotic."

"Is that often?"

She shrugged. "It happens. As with everyone. You, too, sounded a bit odd when I rang. Any reason?"

"I'd been repaying a debt. Someone I knew, someone I'd borrowed from got killed. So yesterday I went and handed the amount to his widow. I'd not been keen on going. I was in a bit of a state."

She nodded sympathetically.

"Last month a friend of mine got killed. Some drunk asked her to his place and strangled her. She'd lent me books from her parents. I still have them. She'd just had her eighteenth birthday. Wonderful spread Mum and Dad put on . . ."

"Change the subject?"

She nodded. Her smile returned.

"Pour me another," she said.

There was not much champagne left, but fortunately I still had a bottle of Hungarian slivovitz.

"To who?" I asked, raising my glass.

"Us."

"We've drunk to us."

"A good toast bears repeating," she said firmly.

It was long after midnight when we went to bed, and near morning when we fell asleep.

27

December

Outside, the crunch of snow and the chill breath of it through the open window vent.

For three days now, to our mutual enjoyment, though probably in different ways, Lena had been woman of the house. Yet every so often came the gloomy thought of how such blissful happiness had more than once ended abruptly, leaving me alone in a flat still filled with her living presence, beseechingly gazing at a silent telephone, as if it could help. A thought I did my best to dispel so as not to let it spoil our celebration. I was sure, watching Lena, that our brief illusion of life together was as much to her liking as to mine.

And when I played the Corelli tape, it was not to calm neurosis, but because tender violins were in harmony with our mutual enjoyment, dispelling nagging thoughts as to its impermanence.

The banality of permanence was what I wanted, and for unremitting happiness, no more than compatibility and togetherness with a woman, as in my Lena idyll, her adherence to some secret timetable the only impediment. An aspiration, which for all I knew, she might share, our time together serving as a palliative to a life I knew nothing of.

I balked at asking more of her. I simply must find something to occupy me during her spells of absence. So long as they *were* only temporary!

"Chips for supper," she declared happily, then looking out of the window, "'Winter, but no peasants celebrating.'" And then from the kitchen, "Did you hear?"

"Yes."

"When *we* studied Nekrasov, I thought the peasants didn't do badly under the Tsar, and winter was when they rested. 'Winter – peasants celebrate' . . ."

"You and your peasants!" I laughed, joining her in the kitchen.

"Can't you just imagine – weeny timber house in the country, smoke curling from the chimney, and us, drinking tea with strawberry jam, snug inside."

"As in 'Masha, me and the samovar'."

To my surprise the telephone rang.

"Tolya?"

"Speaking."

"Marina, Kostya's widow. Sorry to be a nuisance . . . You came, you remember?"

"Of course."

"I don't like asking, but you're my only hope. You couldn't come over at six, could you?"

"I think so," I said warily. "Why?"

"There's something I must go and attend to . . ." she said

eventually. "It'll take a couple of hours . . . And I've no-one to leave Misha with."

"Ah!"

"So, could you?"

"Yes," I said, catching the anxiety in her voice. "At six."

"Oh, thank you."

Putting down the receiver, I stood perplexed.

"Who was that?" asked Lena.

"The widow I took the money to."

"What does she want?"

"Me to baby-sit for a couple of hours."

"*You?*" she laughed. "Good with nappies, are you?"

I didn't think it funny.

"You'll cope," she said, patting me on the back. "How old is it?"

"A few months."

"Can you put up with its crying?"

"No idea."

This intrusion into our temporary little world together was not only destructive of peace and quiet, it brought back the whole business of Kostya. I asked Lena to hold me tight.

"You're trembling – whatever's the matter?" she asked with concern.

For some minutes we stood in each other's arms. Breathing the scent of her hair, I whispered "I love you!"

over and over like a spell, giving no thought to the meaning of the words, calming myself as it were, only to realise half an hour or so later that Lena was for me what Corelli was for her. She was at one and the same time tranquilliser and composure, and my "I love you!" my highest form of gratitude.

I was happy and could smile again, something Lena could not see, being still clasped close to me.

28

Evening

It was dark when I got to Marina's. The instant I pressed the bell the door opened as if she had been waiting by it.

"Glad you could make it," she said. "In five minutes I must go. Come in, take your jacket off. There's a hook – are you warm enough in that? – here are some slippers. Come through to the kitchen. I'll make you a coffee. I'm so glad you've come. I'm so tired, but I simply have to go this evening. I thought of asking one of my girl friends to baby-sit, but not having seen them since the funeral, I was afraid it would just mean memories and tears." Her chatter reflected the hurry she was in.

She was in jeans and a denim jacket over a green sweater,

and for the first time I became aware of brown eyes and, mingled with the aroma from my little ceramic cup, her perfume.

"He has his feed at 7.00. His bottle's here on the radiator. Help yourself from the fridge if you're hungry . . . I'll be back by 8.00. Disposable nappies under the cot, if he cries. It shows on the packet how to change them. It's very simple."

There was just time to show me the little one asleep and breathing heavily in his cot in the living room.

"What if he's still sleeping at 7.00?"

"He won't be. He works to a timetable, like Pavlov's dog. 'Bye."

The door banged and I was alone. The flat was like the one I had grown up in, except that ours had been on the top floor, living room, bedroom, pokey lavatory, pokey bathroom, low whitewashed ceiling dark with damp, kitchen with little window. And under the little window, by tradition, the main item of furniture, the kitchen table with plastic top decorated by some simple-minded designer with pale-green maple leaves, the whole edged in Duralumin to form a trap for breadcrumbs and kitchen muck.

This flat, with its white ceilings and gloss painted doors was much better cared for than mine. Sitting on the sofa, I contemplated the cot, bought for growth, and the tiny bundle that was Misha occupying a third of it. He was asleep. And for just a moment my mind was at ease, as if I, in common with millions of others, was at home with all as it should be – the child as much mine as the Electron TV in the corner between balcony and German dresser with its cut-glass vases, *The Three Musketeers* in three volumes and the Soviet bible, the two-volume Pushkin (print run 2,000,000!), all unread. The moment passed, and there I was in a strange flat, seeing from the alarm clock on top of the TV that there was an hour and 50 minutes to go until 8.00.

Lena would be getting supper. She'd promised chips. How little life altered. Twelve years or so back a girl friend, whose face I could no longer recall, had been fond of frying me chips.

Getting up, I walked around the room, wrote a bold "Hello" in the thin film of dust on the TV, and proceeded to the kitchen, where, finding a packet of Indian tea on a shelf above the stove, I put the kettle on.

Familiarisation with someone else's flat is best begun from the kitchen, and certainly the kitchen was where I felt most at home. Maybe because here, to the right of the window, was where I had sat, having brought the money. The boiling kettle imposed a cosy domestic note over the silence. The windless December evening was loud with trams. The nearest street lamp shone on leafless trees and a white Zhiguli.

When I returned to the living room, the alarm clock showed 6.45. I peered into the cot. He was still asleep.

At 7.00 I fetched his bottle from the kitchen and again bent over him. His eyes were still tight shut. Recalling Marina's "Pavlov's dog", I smiled.

Hungry, I went back to the kitchen, returned the bottle to the radiator, and looking in the fridge, found all I needed – butter, cheese and sausage – but nothing cooked. Topping up the teapot, I made myself a couple of sandwiches and resumed my seat.

The telephone rang in the passage. I went and answered it, but hearing only breathing, hung up. It must have been a wrong number.

Half an hour later I took another look at him. He was still sleeping. I rang Lena and asked her what I should do.

"Don't be neurotic, let sleeping babies lie. He'll tell you when he's hungry. By the bye, potatoes peeled and ready."

"On my way in half an hour."

Silence.

Time dragged on, together with an irritating silence not to be broken for fear of waking one who should long since have been caterwauling to be fed.

I put a hand to his warm cheek, and still he slept, miniature face free of line and feature. Who would he be like? Who was he like now? At this age all babies were the same. I looked around for a photograph of Kostya, but there wasn't one. In fact, there were no photographs anywhere, just books. Still, by her bed would be the place.

Tiptoeing to the bedroom, I switched on the light. Wooden double bed, bedside table with radio, mini alarm clock, round mirror, pile of magazines, and on the pillow a book: Heinrich Böll's *House with no Man*. Strange reading with no photographs of him! But how was the time? The alarm said 8.05. Switching off the light, I went back to the living room. The little wretch was still asleep. No matter, she'd be back any minute, and I, again hungry, would depart to my chips.

So, braving the silence, hoping to hear a key in the lock, I sat, hearing only the tick of the clock on the top of the TV, and becoming increasingly annoyed. Hating me, he was pretending to sleep, not wanting me to feed him! Nonsense, of course, since babies couldn't care less who fed them, so long as somebody did. For a while I was calmer, then, seeing it now to be 8.20, reverted to my former state.

I rang the flat.

"What the hell?" asked Lena.

"Still not back. What do I do?" Speaking to Lena, my annoyance turned to perplexity.

"Some loving mother for you! Hasn't she rung?"

"No."

I could see her by the telephone, shrugging her pretty shoulders.

"Well, you can't leave him, so you'll have to wait, and hungry little me will have to eat and leave some for you."

"Shouldn't I wake him? It's past his feed time."

"Look, I'm no Hero Mother of the Soviet Union, but wake him if you must!"

"See you!" I said, hastening to end our conversation on a peaceable note.

"Love you," she said, hanging up.

This time when I peered into the cot, his eyes were open. Seeing me, he moved his lips. Relieved, I fetched and produced his bottle, expecting a smile. But he merely opened his eyes the wider, and when I put the teat to his lips, seemed not to notice, eyeing me with cold hostility and refusing to suck.

Well, starve, sod you! I thought.

Returning his bottle to the kitchen, I sat at the table. Now, had I still been a smoker, would have been the moment for a cigarette. Failing which, coffee or alcohol. I looked in the fridge. Cognac. Not what I wanted.

The kitchen still held a waft of her perfume which the silence seemed to intensify. Eyes yielding to the day's fatigue, I had an urge to close them, though not to sleep. This flat, this infuriatingly, terrifyingly silent and motionless baby was what they were sick of.

God, what *am* I doing here? I wondered, closing my eyes.

Performing a duty, discharging a debt, God said.

Again?

And yet again. Your owing will endure.

For ever?

Fear not. For so long only as you remember him.

What I wanted was to forget, only the harder I tried, the more vividly was I back in the rain and glint of broken glass in that godforsaken courtyard with, in the yellow eye of a torch, a body.

Pouring cognac from the fridge into a teacup, I swallowed it like medicine.

The round kitchen wall clock said getting on for 10.00.

Cutting myself more sandwiches, I ate, forgetting both baby and Marina. Once, thinking I heard a cry, I stopped, but decided it was an extraneous noise or my imagination. Anyway, I didn't check, but stayed put, safe in the kitchen, pouring more cognac, baby forgotten, debating long and incomprehensibly with myself the question of debt and duty. Only finally to be aroused by a key in the door, and the return of a worried Marina. "Heavens, I'm most terribly sorry, but that's how it went!"

The clock said 12.30, but oddly I felt no resentment.

"Wouldn't take his feed, and I must go," I said, hoping the clock was wrong but doubting it.

"He could have been frightened, being used only to me,"

said Marina. "I ought to have thought. How are you getting home? I got a taxi, after freezing waiting for a bus." Taking my jacket from the hook, I left with a formal "Good night".

It was freezing. No-one was about. None of the passing cars I thumbed stopped.

It was 2.00 before I got home. Lena was asleep.

"Christ, you're cold!" she muttered as I slipped into bed.

29

It was 11.00 or thereabouts when I woke.

The silence told me that I was alone again. This time for how long? The traditional week or longer? Our four days together had been too few. Could her going before I was awake have had anything to do with my late return? My missing supper and her chips would not have upset her – she wasn't that childish – especially knowing where I was and why. Even so, she was still a child liable to crazy ideas and loveable peculiarities. That was what I liked about her.

In the kitchen, a still warm teapot. I looked for a note, but there wasn't one.

Knowing Lena, I wasn't surprised. She lacked the

required mix of romance and sentimentality. Decisiveness, determination, passion: these were Lena's fortes, and one day she might make some weak-willed creature an ideal wife. And she would put up with him for the sake of having somewhere to come back to after each fling . . .

Meanwhile I was alone again, in thrall to expectancy, entirely dependent on the secret timetable that was hers. But that morning I was not especially pained by her abrupt departure, being still sated with her, her kisses, her passion – a peculiar and reassuring satiety.

I would, I decided, take the day very slowly, not go anywhere, and for a start, ran a hot bath and put the kettle on.

*

Several days passed, and I was pleased to find that being alone no longer affected me as it had in the past. Life was no different. Here was the accustomed lull, a time without Lena, but without my feeling aggrieved.

I was, I decided one evening, sitting drinking tea in the kitchen, Pavlov-conditioned to Lena's phonings. More by accident than design perhaps. Though there did seem to be an element of experimentation in our relationship that turned on the dreaded secret timetable. What did she do on the days not spent with me? Walk Kreshchatik Street? Hardly for more than an hour or two, and in this weather, not at all. But where, with the coming of spring and thawing of life, would I be? It did not bear thinking about. Pavlov's dog asked for nothing, merely waited for a bulb to light, as I for a phone call. What a laugh! Still, given that *any* male-female relationship must to some extent be experimental, it wasn't only my reflexes that were conditioned.

30

Next day the silence of my flat was shattered by the telephone.

It was snowing.

The clock showed 12.45.

I was in my chair with the telephone beside me, reading *Correspondence of Mayakovsky and Lili Brik*, looking for love and romance but finding no more than skittish foolishness.

The telephone made me jump. By now my attitude to loneliness had changed completely, my old "enforced solitude" having become more in the nature of voluntary isolation.

My thoughts more with Mayakovsky and his Lili Brik, I picked up the receiver.

"Tolya?"

"Yes."

"Marina. Again to tell you I'm sorry. You did get home?"

"I did."

"Thank God! I was so worried, and I feel so guilty. You wouldn't be free this evening, I suppose?"

"Actually, yes," I said, expecting to be asked to help in some way, and hoping it wasn't to baby-sit!

"Come to supper then. About 7.00."

"Thank you, I'd like to."

Leaving Mayakovsky and Lili Brik forgotten on the sofa I went to the kitchen to make coffee.

Strong coffee, sweetened with the sight of snow slanting past the window. The biological and the geometric with glass in between. Two realms of space, one quite apart from the natural. My own physical as opposed to mental, world, in which I had my being, deciding when and how much fresh air to admit, when to extend day by putting on light, or shorten it by drawing curtains. That, in my limited realm, was Power, a moment of joy, a fleeting "sense of profound satisfaction", to use a cliché beloved of government. Power like that of the tongue, which, if the coffee be bitter, lets hand reach for spoon and sugar, leaving eye to determine the amount. An unperceived, unconscious game concomitant with any action, any desire, desire being itself a manifestation of power, begetting such truisms as "A woman's wish is law", "The customer is always right". The world was made up of desires, one of the most important being the desire to submit, and I thought I knew how that came about. It all began with woman.

I thought of my wife. She left me because I refused to submit to her, finding no joy in so doing, and in the end she found herself a man submissive enough to restore harmony to her life. I was glad for her. Glad for myself. Glad to be liberated. But by nature sensitive, I found solitude as hard to endure as the want of a woman to submit to without being aware of so doing – a torment not unlike Russia's in its want of a good Tsar. That woman, as I saw her, would be sensitive, loving and intelligent enough to make submission a joy.

Loneliness, now less a burden, had become the solitude long enjoyed by monks, a condition favourable to reflection and perfection of self. Though, to be truthful, self-perfection was not my aim, I being of the number who prefer to be taught by life.

Still it snowed.

Drinking my coffee, I reflected further on the nature of desires, pleased with my originality of mind on the subject.

31

That evening, in a half-empty tram and a state of elation I made my way to Marina's, looking out at the wintry city and thinking how nice to be reborn in it with no fear of repeating the mistakes of one's previous existence. I felt more than usually light-hearted. New Year was in the air. It was as if I was heading for some street carnival, or at very least our "National Outing".

With the year nearing its end, tonight's invitation had the feeling of a whole series of celebrations logically culminating in a New Year's Feast. It would have been nice to take a few flowers, but none were to be had on that particular route.

Marina was all smiles. A pair of slippers awaited me.

The table was laid in the living room. Cheese, sliced sausage, everything neatly set out, main course still in the kitchen, bottle of wine waiting for me to open it. No candles.

The cot, I saw, taking a peep while Marina was in the kitchen, had been moved into the bedroom.

I had the strange idea suddenly that it was not Marina I had come to visit, but Kostya, who, being delayed, we had decided not to wait supper for. At which point, pangs of guilt. What was I doing, entering a home that I had destroyed? But the question failed to intimidate, as if I were possessed of some powerful immunity. I was, I recalled, discharging a duty.

At that moment Marina came in with a great dish of rissoles and fried potatoes.

"Oh, dear! I've forgotten the bread."

"I'll cut some," I said, following her out to the kitchen.

She produced a corkscrew, I opened and poured the wine, and we sat down to eat. Reaching for my glass, I was beset with difficulty. To propose a toast would, for all the absence of any sign of mourning, be like cracking a joke at a funeral, I felt again as if Kostya was still alive and about to join us at any minute. Why else would Marina still speak of herself as his wife rather than his widow. My glass was becoming unsteady.

"Well, to the coming New Year!" said Marina, saving the day.

The cheerful clink of glasses eased the tension.

"Would you like some music?"

I nodded.

Fetching a cassette player from the bedroom, she played light jazz.

"OK?"

"Fine."

She wanted, I sensed, to talk, but didn't know how to start, and to obviate a wake-like meal in silence, I refilled our glasses.

"Here's to a good start next year, and none of the old year's bad," I proposed.

"No repeats," she smiled.

"No repeats," I said with feeling.

"I've got so used to silence recently," she said suddenly. "When Kostya died, I thought at first I'd go mad. For a whole week nothing but phone calls. Then, *cut!* Utter silence . . . I cried, then I thought, it's not me that's dead. I'm *alive!* Mourning, photographs, what was the point? The dead were dead, and should show a bit of consideration to the living, not keep reminding . . . Sorry, I shouldn't be talking like this – you knew him. Do pour some wine.

"The fact is that I've spent a lot of time alone," she continued, glass unheeded. "He was constantly away on business. Crimea one minute, Moscow the next. Next year he was going to study law. It was all fixed, he said, the exams were just a formality. He would give up business, while studying, stay at home with me, help with Misha. He had $12,000 put by, enough to last a year or two."

Clearly she had known nothing of his business. Her Kostya and mine were different people, both of them dead.

"So now it's keep going for the sake of Misha," she said, reaching for her glass. "Kostya never talked of his friends, never brought them home, or I might have known you earlier. Maybe that's what makes it easy to say all this. Still, I'm sorry. Let's drink to a happy New Year."

The clink of glasses cut across the much subdued jazz.

The bottle was nearly empty. Time to be going, I thought, just as Misha started crying.

"Won't be a moment," said Marina.

Getting up to stretch my legs, I saw my inscription still in the TV dust.

When she returned, I made as if to go.

"You must have some gâteau – I spent hours making it."

"I returned to the table. With the gâteau went tea and a liqueur in miniature tumblers. It was about midnight when I left. She kissed me on the cheek and told me to ring, writing her number on a pocket calendar – next year's, I saw, when I got home.

32

Snowing on and off, the year moved to its close.

One evening Marina rang asking my address so as to send me a New Year card, and it occurred to me that she might be intending to pop in unexpectedly.

So time to tidy up a bit. Starting with the ubiquitous newspapers and magazines, I set to work, and within the hour achieved a more pronounced aura of civilisation that extended to dusted surfaces. Now the question was whether she would come, if so, when, and hopefully not to coincide with Lena. Two days passed and nobody came, but on the third there was a letter.

Dear Tolya,

Thank you for coming. I greatly enjoyed our supper and the human warmth of it. It's ages since I got anyone a meal. It's dull cooking just for yourself. It would be nice to have a repeat. You are, I'm sure, much sought after. Even so, I'd like to invite you for a quiet New Year celebration – you're such good company, so kind and attentive. If you have other plans don't worry – just ring and say. Marina.

I had, I realised, given no thought to New Year, counting, though without having consulted her, on celebrating *à deux* with Lena. It was a week since she had rung. So I would hear, if not today, tomorrow, barring some radical change in her timetable.

I played Corelli. There was a breath of spring about the music, as if this year was done, all that was bad forgotten, and a new life, a fresh start in the making. One good thing after another, smiles all the way, thoughts, actions, all bathed in romance. A world that was ideal, naïf, a world I lived in and was in keeping with. Some kindly, unseen censor having excised the grey and the black of life's experience, and left me as fine and upstanding as any hero of Soviet classical literature – even if deficient in heroic spirit and deed, and totally devoid of enthusiasm for, or pride in, my native land, or a people of which I had no knowledge. A world in which all were united by a happy past.

As I re-read her note, it occurred to me that there was more to it than an invitation to a New Year supper. Her "kind and attentive" was pleasing. Flattered and grateful, I could not help thinking of Dima's disparaging "Another will take his place". Well, I'd happily worn his slippers. They fitted. And if someone always did take someone's place, why shouldn't it be me?

33

With a week to go, Kiev put up New Year decorations to distract from the daily grind, children were playing "civil war", fighting with snowballs, and the radio was broadcasting promises from on high that the price of bread and milk would not be "liberalised".

Lena turned up at last with a bottle of champagne and a box tied with festive ribbon. "A New Year's present," she said.

I kissed and thanked her. "Open now or wait till New Year?"

"Up to you."

"How about New Year? What are we doing?"

"Let's leave that till tomorrow."

When, at supper, she toasted the New Year, I felt sure we would not be seeing it in together, but said nothing, determined to put on a brave face, and make the most of what I had.

It was morning before we slept, and midday when we woke.

I went to the kitchen and made coffee.

Back under the blankets and reaching down for my cup of coffee on the floor, I asked again about New Year.

"No good," she sighed. "I'm booked for a bankers' 'mini Decameron'."

"A what?"

"Orgy with group sex. I'm looking to the future, saving for a one-roomer."

I nodded, smiling at the literary ring of mini Decameron! There was always a word for everything, and if there wasn't, one got invented.

My problem of choice was removed.

Before she left, Lena made me open my parcel. Socks. Of all colours.

"To last you the year. When I'm next here, your holey ones go out of the window!"

When she had gone, I rang Marina, thanked her for her invitation and said I would come.

Next morning I went to buy her a New Year present, visiting boutiques, shops, seeing what other men were buying.

I had the feeling of entering on a new, quiet, stable, comfortable life, such as I had aspired to.

In three months little Misha would be sitting on my knee saying Da-da, and nothing he said thereafter would ever match that for importance.

My old schoolfriend Dima would turn up, and help to invest Kostya's $12,000 in something earning good interest.

Marina and I would embark on a quiet and happy bourgeois existence, meeting new friends and avoiding old.

I would give the keys of my one-roomer to Lena and sometimes we would chat on the phone.

Life would be good, and I would be completely won over by it.

EPILOGUE

Some days after our quiet celebration of New Year – I having at Marina's insistence moved in with her – a postcard arrived requesting payment in respect of a post office box, which was, I saw with a start, the very one where I had deposited the envelope of info. for Kostya. I thought instantly of the carrier bag still at my flat containing what I had taken from Kostya's pockets. The key to the box might well be amongst them. I hurried off to check, and finding that it was, proceeded to the post office.

The box contained an envelope addressed to Kostya, which I pocketed, then having paid rental for a further year, I crunched my way through the snow to St Andrew's Church and down the Descent to Fraternal Street and my café. Here, over a cup of double strength at my favourite table, I examined the contents of the envelope: passport photo of a man aged about 50, neat hair, suit, collar and tie, and written on the back, "10.01. Spadshchina, Podol, 6.00 pm."

*

The Spadshchina was a restaurant, and on January 10, I went, with strange feelings, to Podol. I tried to think of myself as Kostya doing the same, but could not manage to at all. My mind was totally confused. It was, I realised, me who was Kostya, wearing his slippers, going daily to the dairy on his son's behalf . . . The last three months had turned everything on its head. And today it was as if the remote past had come alive again, stirring doubts afresh. What if Kostya were alive? Alive was what one was so long as no-one knew anything to the contrary. The person who had deposited the envelope could have known nothing of Kostya's death. So here was I heading for a restaurant selected for a killing that would not take place because the would-be killer was dead. There was a touch of theatre about it. What I wanted was to have a look at the man not going to be killed today, and oblivious of the chance happenings on which his survival depended. Which was not to say that he might not be killed tomorrow elsewhere, by someone else.

I arrived at the snug little restaurant on the early side at 5.30. It was only just open after the afternoon break, and the waiter wasn't expecting custom so soon.

Twenty minutes or so later, the man arrived and was shown to a table facing mine.

I was struck by the utter theatricality of it: play for two actors and one waiter, the latter as sole but invisible audience. Never did the avant-garde want for novelty. Watching closely, I could see from the unsteadiness of the menu he was holding that his hands were shaking. Was he, I wondered, aware of the danger he was in?

Seeing me looking, he looked back. The coloured

lighting made it impossible to determine his expression.

The waiter served wine and *hors d'oeuvres*. Reality, as I sipped my red wine, was now more that of the cinema.

A decanter of vodka and *hors d'oeuvres* were brought for him. The waiter poured obligingly, took a step back and froze pending a curt nod from the diner, clearly long one of life's managers. Accompanying the nod, a look of something between contempt and studied indifference directed at me. Still staring, he got to his feet, took two steps towards me, and collapsed, clutching at his heart, eyes raised to the low ceiling.

"Call an ambulance!" I instructed the waiter who came bounding in at the noise.

He did so, and when he returned, bent and examined the man, and I joined him.

"He's dead," said the waiter incredulously. "Heart attack," he added with a shrug.

I collected my jacket and left.

It was dark and still snowing.

I walked quickly to the metro, clutching the postbox key in my pocket, conscious of the killer inside me, but undismayed.